W9-AUB-095

3 2306 00691 9149

AG - - '14

DISCARD

PROPERTY OF C L P L

The Lake Where Loon Lives

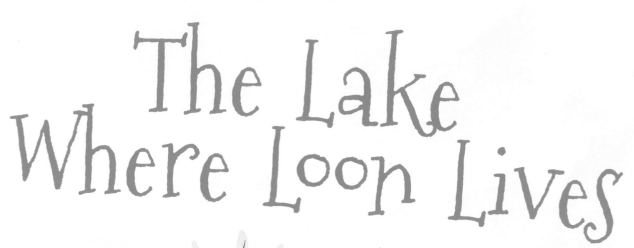

WRITTEN BY

Brenda Reeves Sturgis

ILLUSTRATED BY

Brooke Carlton

books@islandportpress.com   www.islandportpress.com

Text copyright © 2014 by Brenda Reeves Sturgis
Illustrations copyright © 2014 by Brooke Carlton

All rights reserved. No part of this book may be reproduced in any manner without the express written consent of Islandport Press
except in the case of brief excerpts in critical reviews and articles.

Printed in the United States by Versa Press
ISBN: 978-1-939017-24-6

Library of Congress Control Number: 2013922641

To my littlest loons, Seabren, Landen, Sondre, Hannah, and Chace, and to my agent Karen G., who always has my back.
BRENDA REEVES STURGIS

For Erin, who has the patience of Job, the wisdom of Jesus, and the delightful conviction that much can be salved with a decent slab of dark chocolate.
BROOKE CARLTON

ISLANDPORT PRESS

Islandport Press, P.O. Box 10, Yarmouth, Maine 04096
books@islandportpress.com
www.islandportpress.com

This is the lake where Loon lives.

This is Loon, who glides outside,

here on the lake where Loon lives.

These are her **wings** that are stretched open wide,

that span the loon who glides outside,
here on the lake where Loon lives.

These are her **feathers**
daubed white and black,

layered on wings that are stretched open wide,
that span the loon who glides outside,
here on the lake where Loon lives.

These are Loon's **chicks**
who ride on her back,

Wet Paint

resting on feathers daubed white and black,
which are layered on wings that are stretched open wide,
that span the loon who glides outside,
here on the lake where Loon lives.

These are Loon's eyes

watching the chicks who ride on her back,
as they're resting on feathers daubed white and black,
which are layered on wings

brilliant and red,

that are stretched open wide,
that span the loon who glides outside,
here on the lake where Loon lives.

This is the **fly** who circles Loon's head,

above beady eyes so brilliant and red,
watching the chicks who ride on her back,
as they're resting on feathers
daubed white and black,
which are layered on wings
that are stretched open wide,
that span the loon who glides outside,
here on the lake where Loon lives.

This is the **fish** who snaps at the fly,

which bothers and circles around Loon's head,
above beady eyes so brilliant and red,
watching the chicks who ride on her back,
as they're resting on feathers daubed white and black,
which are layered on wings that are stretched open wide,
that span the loon who glides outside,
here on the lake where Loon lives.

This is the bOY on the dock passing by;

he studies the fish who snaps at the fly,
which bothers and circles around Loon's head,
above beady eyes so brilliant and red,
 watching the chicks who ride on her back,
  as they're resting on feathers
   daubed white and black,
    which are layered on wings
     that are stretched open wide,
      that span the loon who
       glides outside,
        here on the lake
         where Loon lives.

This is the line that is cast to the fish,

by the boy on the dock who is currently dry,
as he studies the fish who snaps at the fly,
which bothers and circles around Loon's head,
above beady eyes so brilliant and red,
watching the chicks who ride on her back,

as they're resting on feathers
daubed white and black,
which are layered on wings
that are stretched open wide,
that span the loon who glides outside,
here on the lake where Loon lives.

This is the **struggle**, the **swish**, and the **splash**,

made by the flopping, the flip, and the thrash,
as the boy on the dock who is no longer dry
reels in the fish who snaps at the fly,
which bothers and circles around Loon's head
above beady eyes so brilliant and red,

watching the chicks who ride on her back,
as they're resting on feathers daubed white and black,
which are layered on wings that are stretched open wide,
that span the loon that glides outside,
here on the lake where Loon lives.

This is the **spot** where
Loon stops to rest,

escaping the struggle, the splash, and the swish,
made by the line that was cast to the fish,
by the boy off the dock who is drenched, "OH MY!"
and the feisty fish who snapped at the fly,
which bothers and circles around Loon's head,
above beady eyes so brilliant and red,
watching the chicks who ride on her back,
as they're resting on feathers daubed white and black,
which are layered on wings that are stretched open wide,
that span the loon who glides outside,
here on the lake where Loon lives.

This is the **time** that Loon loves best,

at the spot near her nest, where she stops to rest,
escaping the struggle, the splash, and the swish,
made by the line that was cast to the fish,
by the boy off the dock who is drenched, "OH MY!"
and the feisty fish who snapped at the fly.

But the boy, the fish, and the fly go away,
and Loon is content at the end of the day,
watching her chicks, not making a peep,
snuggled by feathers and ready for sleep,
in wings that cuddle and tuck in tight
as Loon wails out to all...

Good night!
Here on the lake where Loon lives.

ABOUT THE AUTHOR

Brenda Reeves Sturgis is a Maine author who began her writing journey in 2004 after attending a school visit by author Lynn Plourde. She is the author of *10 Turkeys in the Road* and *No Fun in the Sun for Santa*. She and her husband Gary live on a lovely little lake where she listens to loons wail and watches an occasional moose meander across her back yard. She has four children and five grandchildren.

ABOUT THE ILLUSTRATOR

Brooke Carlton began drawing as an excuse to color in her own picture book ideas. She arbitrarily chose pen and ink, with an old set of Winsor & Newton watercolors to fill in. The resulting combo and hot palette quickly became her trademark. Her whimsical illustrations have appeared in children's magazine and book publications, private home collections, commercial brochures and posters, mailing envelopes, and even large mural walls. In addition to doing illustration work, she is also a musician. With paintbrush in one hand, saxophone in the other, and her dog, Lucy, at her feet, Brooke works out of her tiny studio in the woods of rural Maine.